Brita Orstadius

THE DOLPHIN JOURNEY

Pictures by Lennart Didoff

Translated by Eric Bibb

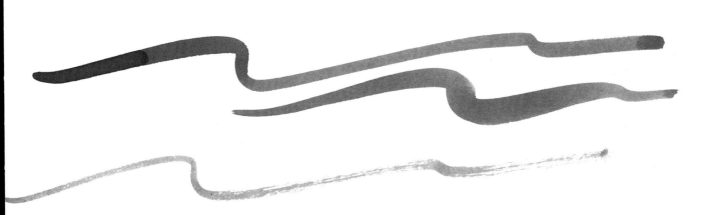

R&S
BOOKS

Stockholm   New York   Toronto   London   Adelaide

Pia and Ianni are best friends. They are both six years old. Pia's mother and father are Swedish. She has big blue eyes, which are always full of laughter, and a lot of freckles on her little button nose. Her thick ponytail is so blond it's almost white.

Ianni's parents are Greek, but he and his little sister were born in Sweden. He has two older brothers who were born in Greece. Ianni has curly jet-black hair that sticks straight up in the air, and the most wonderful black eyes. At least, Pia thinks they are wonderful. When she jokes around with Ianni, his eyes grow as bright as a bird's.

Pia and Ianni live in the same building. They've always known each other. They've played in the same sandbox and slid down the same slide. They've gone to the same kindergarten.

Pia doesn't have any brothers or sisters. Instead, she has Ianni and his brothers and little sister.

One day, Ianni's mother said to Pia's mother: "We're going to Greece this summer. Our relatives on the island haven't met our Swedish-born children."

"Oh, a Greek island," said Pia's mother. "That sounds wonderful. I've seen on television how beautiful it is in Greece."

Ianni's mother said that if they wanted to come along, they could rent Ianni's grandmother's little house. And so it was decided that they'd all travel to Greece together. Pia and Ianni jumped for joy.

Finally, the big day arrived. It was the first time that Pia and
Ianni had been on an airplane, and they both had butterflies in
their stomachs. The plane's engines thundered. Suddenly it
started to move. The next moment, they were off the ground.
Treetops flew by outside the windows. Soon the airplane was
floating high in the blue sky. When they looked down at the
ground, the cars looked like tiny beetles. The houses were no
bigger than building blocks, and the ground was checkered yellow
and green. Clouds swirled around the plane like giant rabbit tails,
all white and fluffy.

They flew for several hours. They saw mountaintops sparkling white with snow, and lakes that looked like blue-green bowls.

Finally they landed in a big city bathed in a yellow haze. The air was so hot that they could barely breathe as they stepped out of the plane. It smelled of pine sap and dust.

Ianni's uncle came to pick them up in a little bus. He drove them to the sea. Wherever they looked, they were surrounded by water in the most beautiful color that Pia had ever seen. Blue-blue-blue, she thought. Then they rode out to sea aboard a little boat. The boat was crowded with people and sheep and a rooster and a pig and chickens in cages. They passed many islands.

One island was as flat as a plate; another was as pointed as a
magician's hat. Then they saw a completely white island. When
they came closer, they saw that it was the houses on the island
that were shining like white sugar cubes under the bright blue sky.

The boat sailed into port. Many people, both young and old, and
even dogs and cats, came running from the houses. Up on the cliffs
you could see goats and sheep. Everyone was happy to see the boat.
People laughed and shouted and hugged and kissed. Some cried
with happiness. The sun shone over everything like a huge lemon.

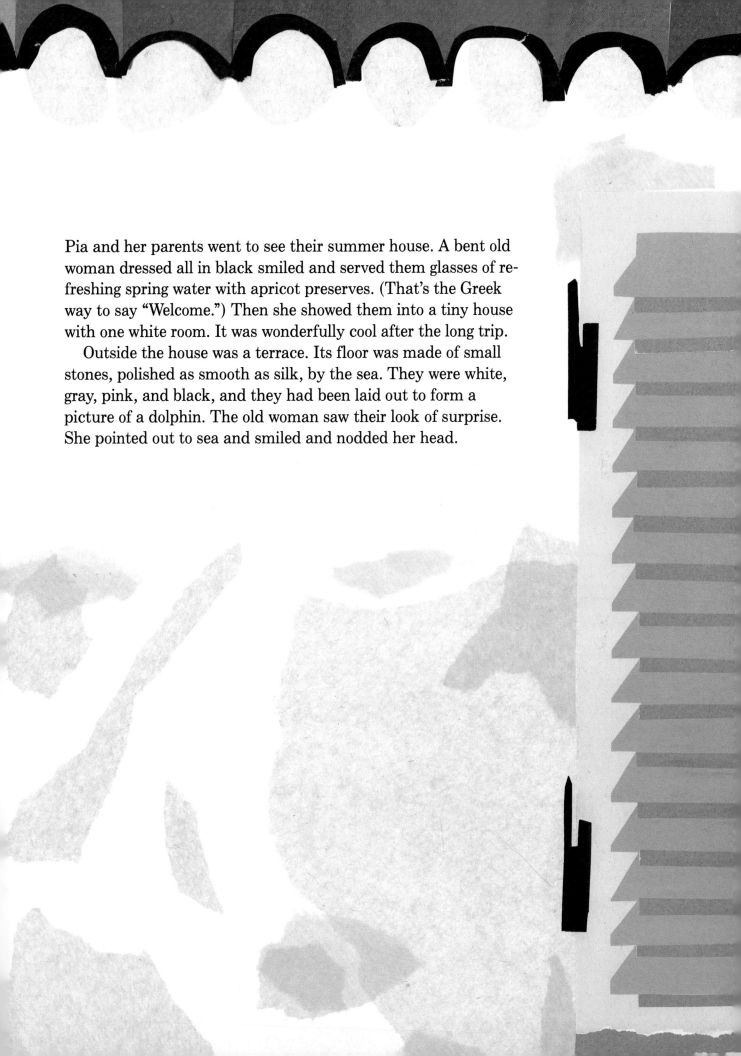

Pia and her parents went to see their summer house. A bent old woman dressed all in black smiled and served them glasses of refreshing spring water with apricot preserves. (That's the Greek way to say "Welcome.") Then she showed them into a tiny house with one white room. It was wonderfully cool after the long trip.

Outside the house was a terrace. Its floor was made of small stones, polished as smooth as silk, by the sea. They were white, gray, pink, and black, and they had been laid out to form a picture of a dolphin. The old woman saw their look of surprise. She pointed out to sea and smiled and nodded her head.

The sun was setting. For a few minutes it hung like a big red planet above the horizon. Then it appeared to be no more than a slice of watermelon. Finally it slipped behind the farthest edge of the earth, and darkness covered the island like a soft piece of velvet.

In Greece, dinner is eaten late in the evening. Everyone sat up on the roof, where there were cool breezes. Over the laughter and the singing around the table, you could hear the sound of the sea. After dinner, all the children fell asleep in a corner, but the grown-ups sang and danced far into the night.

The village lay high up on the island's cliffs. Down below was a little round cove with fine white sand. A winding path led to the beach through a tunnel of fragrant bushes and birdsong. The children went swimming at the cove every day. They built sand castles and searched for shells.

One morning Pia and Ianni went down to the beach early, but
Ianni's brother Niko was already there.

"Look," said Niko, pointing out to sea. They saw a boat on its
way to the island. Around the boat, large fish were rolling in the
water. They looked like huge wheels.

"Those aren't fish," said Niko. "Those are dolphins, playing in
the boat's wake."

The dolphins jumped. Their mouths opened as if they were
laughing, and they made a high whistling sound.

"Let's go in," said Niko. "Maybe they'll come this way." Pia and Ianni stayed close to shore. After the hot sand, the sea felt cool and soothing. They waded out on the sandy bottom.

Niko swam out into deeper water; he turned over and floated on his back. The boat and the dolphins had disappeared. The water was very still.

Then a huge wave came and turned Niko over on his side. He rolled around, and along came another wave. They felt like the after-waves that come from a passing boat, but there was no boat. There was only Pia and Ianni and Niko. Niko began swimming toward the shallow water where Pia and Ianni were hunting for seashells. A new wave came and turned him upside down. He swallowed a lot of water. Now he was afraid. Suddenly there were bubbles in the water all around him. He felt something nudge against his leg — something smooth and slippery. It felt as if a large body had passed by.

Niko struggled to the surface and saw something streak across the water. It made a wide arc across the cove and turned toward shore again.

"A shark!" cried Niko. "Run, Pia and Ianni. Run!"

Pia and Ianni tried to run, but it wasn't easy. The water reached up to their waists. Niko caught up with them.

Now the creature was swimming toward them with great speed. The surface was parted by a broad shiny black back. They saw a dark back fin and a huge shining eye. Then the animal sank again. An incoming wave lifted the children, and they floated in toward shore.

"That wasn't a shark," said Ianni.

"No, because sharks have fins like knives," said Pia.

"And it had a kind eye like a seal's," said Niko.

"Imagine if it was a dolphin," said Pia. "Maybe he wants to come play with us."

Just then, the animal came swimming in their direction again, landing in the shallow water with a great thud. He was huge and shiny as he lay there in the clear water, rocking from side to side. His eyes were friendly, and his beak-like nose continued into a wide smile. He didn't seem at all afraid. He breathed noisily through the airhole on his head and splashed with his large tail fin.

The dolphin dove and disappeared. But a few minutes later the surface parted and he flew up in the air with a great leap. The sound of his tail fin smacking the water was like a shot. Then he was gone.

What an adventure! The children didn't tell anyone. But every morning they went down to the beach. And every morning the dolphin came and played with Niko. By now, Pia and Ianni also dared to swim farther out.

One day, while they were playing, Ianni suddenly disappeared.

"Niko, Ianni's gone!" screamed Pia.

Niko dove, but he couldn't find Ianni.

"Help! Help!" shouted Pia and Niko. Many of the villagers heard them and came running down to the beach.

Then along came a big wave with Ianni floating on its crest. Niko
caught hold of him and held on tight. They struggled up onto the
beach together. It was the dolphin who had saved Ianni. He had
felt its smooth skin lift him to the surface.

After that, the children were told not to play with the dolphin
anymore. But he came every morning and played by himself.
They got a whistle, and when they blew it, the dolphin jumped
with joy and laughed at them.

One night, it was unusually hot. Pia couldn't sleep. She crept up
to the roof and sat looking at the beach and the sea and the stars.
She heard a whisper from the neighbor's roof. It was Ianni, who
couldn't sleep either.

  "Look at that big rock on the beach."

  "That's not a rock," said a voice from the corner. It was Niko,
who had been sleeping on the roof.

  "It just moved. Let's go look."

  The children got a flashlight and ran down to the beach. They
shone a light on the rock-like shape.

It was the dolphin. He was alive. He looked at them with kind
sad eyes and wiggled his tail fin a little. He didn't seem to be
hurt, but he wasn't as wet as he should be.

"It's the same with whales," said Niko. "They can come up on
land for a while, but they have to get back in the water quickly or
their skin begins to crack."

"We have to get help," said Pia, "or he'll die."

Ianni woke his father up. His father woke up the whole village.
People came running. A fisherman cleaned out the dolphin's airhole. It was full of sand. Its next breath came as a great warm
puff, and the big body trembled. He smelled of salt and seaweed,
but his skin was rough and dry like sandpaper.

The mothers and grandmothers and children ran to get buckets of water to pour over the dolphin. Pia protected his airhole with her hand. The fathers and grandfathers dug out the sand around the dolphin and tried to move him, but he was too heavy. He lay there like a huge block of stone.

"He must weigh more than five hundred pounds," said Ianni's father. The sky began to get lighter. Soon the sun would be up, and the dolphin would be scorched. One of the island's fishing boats still lay anchored near land. The others were already out fishing. The men managed to tie a rope around the dolphin just behind the back fin. They tied it to other lengths of rope until it reached out to the anchored boat, which could not come nearer to shore.

They all pulled. A few of the men took off their pants and stood ready to follow the dolphin out into the water, where they would cut the rope.

The boat's motor began to chug. The dolphin seemed completely relaxed. He wasn't frightened of the boat, which slowly began to move. The rope rose out of the water and tightened. When the boat began to tug, the rope dug into the dolphin's skin.

A tremor passed through the big body. The dolphin began slowly sliding across the sand toward the water's edge. You could hear small shells being crushed under his weight. He reached the water, but he didn't move at all.

Pia bit her lip.

"What if he's dead," she whispered to Ianni.

The men turned the body so that the head faced out to sea. The dolphin seemed paralyzed. Then the men felt his muscles start to work. A forefin flapped gently in the water. They began to cut the thick rope.

Just as they cut through the rope, the dolphin's muscles tensed; the airhole closed, and he shot forward and dove. The men lost their balance in the undertow. Laughing and spitting water, they helped each other to their feet. A great cheer went up from the shore. Everyone shouted with relief, because dolphins have always been considered holy in the islands. Far off, the dolphin leapt above the waves. He looked like a golden wheel in the morning sun.

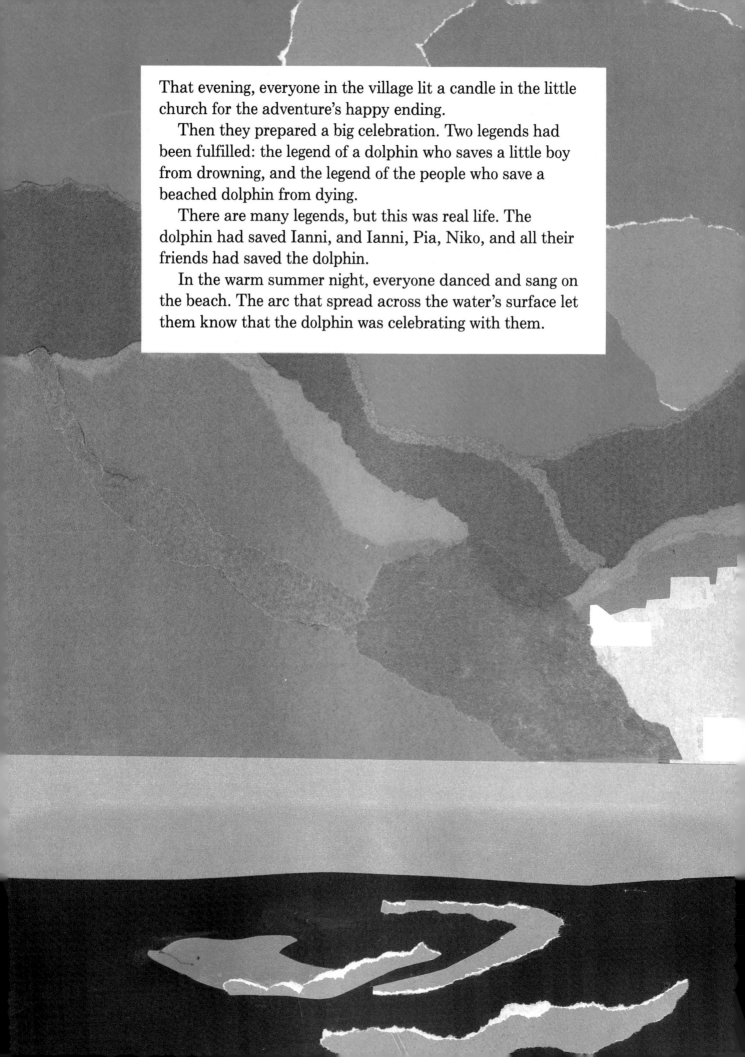

That evening, everyone in the village lit a candle in the little church for the adventure's happy ending.

Then they prepared a big celebration. Two legends had been fulfilled: the legend of a dolphin who saves a little boy from drowning, and the legend of the people who save a beached dolphin from dying.

There are many legends, but this was real life. The dolphin had saved Ianni, and Ianni, Pia, Niko, and all their friends had saved the dolphin.

In the warm summer night, everyone danced and sang on the beach. The arc that spread across the water's surface let them know that the dolphin was celebrating with them.

Rabén & Sjögren Stockholm

Translation copyright © 1989 by Eric Bibb
All rights reserved
Illustrations copyright © 1987 by Lennart Didoff
Text copyright © 1987 by Brita Orstadius
Originally published in Sweden by Rabén & Sjögren
under the title *Delfinresan.*
Library of Congress catalog card number: 88-23973
Printed in Denmark, 1989
First edition, 1989

ISBN 91 29 59138 4

R & S Books are distributed in the United States of America
by Farrar, Straus and Giroux, New York;
in Canada by General Publishing, Toronto;
in the United Kingdom by ragged Bears, Andover;
and in Australia by ERA Publications, Adelaide